3

H

J Abdo X
Abdo, Kenny
Triple take

TRIPLE TAKE

BY **KENNY ABDO**

ILLUSTRATED BY **BOB DOUCET**

visit us at www.abdopublishing.com

Published by Magic Wagon, a division of the ABDO Group,
PO Box 398166, Minneapolis, Minnesota 55439. Copyright © 2014
by Abdo Consulting Group, Inc. International copyrights reserved in all
countries. All rights reserved. No part of this book may be reproduced
in any form without written permission from the publisher.

Calico Chapter Books™ is a trademark and logo of Magic Wagon.

Printed in the United States of America, North Mankato, Minnesota.
062013
092013

 This book contains at least 10% recycled materials.

Text by Kenny Abdo
Illustrations by Bob Doucet
Edited by Karen Latchana Kenney
Cover and interior design by Colleen Dolphin, Mighty Media, Inc.

Library of Congress Cataloging-in-Publication Data

Abdo, Kenny, 1986-
  Triple take / Kenny Abdo ; illustrated by Bob Doucet.
       p. cm. – (Haven't got a clue!)
  Summary: On a fourth-grade trip to a local battle site park, Jon
Gummyshoes, fourth-grade detective, learns that sometimes history
should rest in peace when he and Mac investigate a tale of ghosts and
lost gold.
  ISBN 978-1-61641-955-4
1. School field trips–Juvenile fiction. 2. Historical reenactments–Juvenile
fiction. 3. Treasure troves–Juvenile fiction. 4.   Elementary schools–
Juvenile fiction. [1. Mystery and detective stories. 2. School field trips–
Fiction. 3. Historical reenactments–Fiction. 4. Buried treasure–Fiction.
5. Elementary schools–Fiction. 6. Schools–Fiction.] I. Doucet, Bob, ill.
II. Title.
  PZ7.A1589334Tri 2013
  813.6–dc23
                                            2013001070

Table of Contents

The Usual Suspects 4

Note from the Detective's Files........................... 6

CHAPTER 1: Quite the Trip 8

CHAPTER 2: On the Battlefield.................... 15

CHAPTER 3: Stuck in a Plastic Past...........24

CHAPTER 4: See You in the Future 33

CHAPTER 5: Entering the Black Forest.....38

CHAPTER 6: Like Owner, Like Dog............47

CHAPTER 7: Getting into Character..........54

CHAPTER 8: Where the Gold Lies..............62

CHAPTER 9: Let History Rest in Peace 69

CHAPTER 10: Good as Gold 75

A Page from Gummyshoes's Notebook..........80

The Usual Suspects

THE WHO'S WHO OF THE CASE

JON
GUMMYSHOES

LAWRENCE
"LARRY"
MACGUFFIN

PRINCIPAL
LINKS

FRANKIE
FLATS

T-BONE

MR. HANNA

Note from the Detective's Files

The name is Gummyshoes—Jon Gummyshoes.
I know what you're thinking: funny name, right?
Well, that's not what I'm here to talk about. I'm
here to tell you the facts. The cold, hard facts
about the cases I come across day in and day out
at Edwin West Elementary School.

The way I see it, trouble seems to find me
around every corner. So I make it my business to
clean it up. I don't need this game. It needs me.

The case I'm about to share with you wasn't
my first, and it certainly won't be my last. It
was all about history—the history of a town, its
battles, and its long lost gold. I went on a ghost
hunt through a haunted forest. And I found out
that things are never as simple as they seem. It
was a case that I'll never forget.

CHAPTER 1

Quite the Trip

The fourth grade students of Edwin West Elementary and Edwin East Elementary arrived at Triple Crest on separate buses just before nine a.m. Both schools were there on a trip to study the historical Battle of Triple Crest. We had been studying the battle in third period social studies. It was a subject I was not entirely in love with. No, I was only interested in my detective work.

I rode on the Edwin West Elementary school

bus. But I was familiar with Edwin East after a brief stint as their resident detective. My best pal, Larry MacGuffin, and yours truly investigated cases at both schools.

Principal Links and Principal Ant were each chaperoning his school's bus. I discovered a while ago that they used to be classmates, but they had not spoken to each other in years. I decided this trip would be a fine time to figure out that mystery.

Both Principal Links and Principal Ant guided their students off the buses. We stepped out and inhaled the fresh air. I was not usually a fan of field trips, but for some odd reason I felt like this would be a good one.

There were three things that I noticed when we arrived at Triple Crest. First, I noticed that Triple Crest was surrounded by mountains. Second, there was a coffee shop at every corner and every single one had a line out the door. Apparently the coffee was really good here. And finally, there was a giant waterfall right behind the Triple Crest Hotel. I mean that if you took a step out the back door, well, you'd better bring a life jacket.

MacGuffin was stretching after sitting for so long. He had been stuck with Frankie Flats on the bus.

"Hey, Mac, good trip?" I asked.

"About as good as any trip can go crammed into a seat with Frankie Flats. That kid does not stop talking about you."

I opened my backpack and pulled out two walkie-talkies.

"I brought along our walkie-talkies, just in case we need them during this trip," I told Mac. "I just put fresh batteries in, so we should be good if we get separated."

"Thanks," MacGuffin said, grabbing a walkie-talkie. "Hey, by the way, what happened with your dog, Little Ricky? He was locked up or something?"

I let out a disappointed sigh. "Yeah, some joker by the name of Animal Control Officer Tommy Donkers nabbed him. He gave Little Ricky the pinch for digging up the flowers in front of City Hall," I said. "I wish I could prove he didn't do the crime. Little Ricky isn't into public destruction. It just isn't his style. But when I go out looking for clues, I usually let him off his leash so he can do his own thing. So he got picked up for not having a license, too." I blew out some more air. "And boy, it's going to cost me a pretty penny to get him out."

Principal Ant walked up to the rowdy crowd of kids. "All right, students, let's all face here," he said with his hand raised. "Now we are just on the peak of Triple Crest. The great Battle of Triple Crest and many other historical wonders have occurred right where we are standing!" He looked around to see that he'd lost our attention. "But I will leave it to the tour guide to tell us more exciting tales."

"Thank you, Marcus," Principal Links said to Principal Ant. "Now, everyone grab a battle buddy and follow us."

We all followed the principals onto the battlefield.

"Teddy Plugg said this place is haunted something fierce," Frankie Flats said, pushing between me and MacGuffin. "Ya know, haunted from the battles and such. So, what do you think, Gummyshoes? Can you solve that case?"

I stopped and looked at Frankie. "Oh, Frankie, we don't waste our time and talents on cases involving spooks and ghouls. We are dedicated to the here and now. We like cases that are grounded in reality." I threw my hands up and laughed.

"I don't know, Jon," MacGuffin said, stepping forward. "I wouldn't rule anything out quite yet. I mean, who knows what we'll find on this trip. Maybe we'll encounter some real-life ghosts!"

I shifted my attention from Frankie to MacGuffin. "If they are real life, then how are they ghosts?" My eyes went back to Frankie and I smiled wide.

MacGuffin gave me a knock on the shoulder. "We'll look into it, Frankie," he said.

Frankie stared at me for a moment and walked off talking to himself. I looked over at MacGuffin, who just shrugged.

Yes indeed, I thought, *this will be quite the trip*.

CHAPTER 2
On the Battlefield

Soon we were standing in the middle of a field. It looked like frozen mud with hay on it. I kept my hands in my pockets to keep warm. I had remembered to bring my walkie-talkies but forgot my mittens. I should have just let my mom clip them to my jacket sleeves like she wanted to do.

A man wearing a fleece jacket and sandals was standing in front of us. "Hello, children, my name is Anthony. But everyone here calls me T-Bone," he said. He adjusted the sunglasses that were sitting on top of his head. "I will be guiding you through the exciting and incredibly deep history of Triple Crest. As you look around," he motioned with his hands, "you see vast land and mountains. But did you know that one of the most important battles on US soil was fought right here?"

I turned to MacGuffin and whispered, "So what do you think? This place isn't haunted … right? I mean, that stuff is for kids."

I looked back up at T-Bone who was staring right at me. I waited a second and he rolled his eyes back to the crowd.

"Come closer, children. I am going to take you on a journey way back in time. The United States was not yet a decade old. Despite its Revolutionary War victory against the British Empire, the country was still trying to put itself back together. It had its land and many resources, but there was one thing that many people did not know about."

Frankie raised his hand.

"Yes, little boy?" T-Bone asked.

"What was it that not many people knew about?" Frankie asked.

"I'm getting there." T-Bone continued to walk toward a row of trees that led into a forest. "We did not have colonies to squeeze gold and treasure from like the empires of Europe. We did not have a frightening navy or army that could make lofty demands of anyone." He turned around to the trees. "But we had forests." Frankie took a picture of a tree. T-Bone turned around and motioned to the field behind us. "And we had rich soil." Frankie got a shot of the empty field. "We had creativity, courage, and hope."

Frankie raised his hand again.

"What is it?" T-Bone said.

"How is the land rich? It looks kind of crummy to me." Frankie said, looking around.

T-Bone looked confused about Frankie's question. Olivia Pumpernickel, the class know-it-all, sighed and raised her hand. "Mr. T-Bone,

I'll field this. Frankie, back then there was a lot of land and forest that other countries wanted. That is why it was rich. So General Kettle, the hero of Triple Crest, taught the townsfolk how to protect what was theirs." Olivia turned around to Principal Ant and smiled, "I got an A+ on our social studies quiz last week."

"That's right, little girl," T-Bone responded to Olivia. "But nobody likes a know-it-all." Olivia sneered at him and T-Bone moved on. "Triple Crest had the land and the trees, which made it appealing to build a life here." T-Bone sighed and walked us into what looked like a really, really old town.

"So the settlers created a town right here in Triple Crest. Little did they know, Triple Crest was built on top of gold—lots and lots of gold. Only one person knew where the gold was located. That person was General Kettle. But rumors spread about the gold. Pirates soon came to Triple Crest to try to steal it. But the fine citizens of Triple Crest were not going to let their town be invaded without a fight. They were not going to become prisoners of their gold."

We walked by a man wearing a big black apron. He was hammering a big piece of steel on top of an anvil. We saw an old woman sweeping the ground with a straw broom.

"When the pirates arrived in Triple Crest, they were met with not just village people and farmers, but also warriors." T-Bone picked up a piece of steel out of a water cauldron. "Instead of horseshoes, the blacksmiths forged swords. Instead of shoeing the horses, the farriers created walls for defense."

T-Bone dropped the steel, grabbed Frankie Flats by the shirt, and looked him square in the eye. "And everyone else made sure that nobody was going to steal this land." Frankie let out a gulp. T-Bone let go of his shirt and scanned the rest of the crowd. "Now, let's go this way to the enchanted Triple Take Falls!"

We walked through the tiny town, following close to T-Bone. The people who were playing the townsfolk were really in character. We approached a young boy whose head and wrists were trapped between two large, hinged wooden boards. He was wearing old-timey clothes and a hat that was almost falling off.

"Uh oh, looks like another common thief has been caught stealing milk from local barns!" T-Bone said, stopping in front of the boy. "Back then these devices, called stocks, were used as a public form of punishment. Usually they made an example out of young people like this chap. Isn't that right, Evan?"

Evan tried to look up at everyone. "Can I get out of here? My shift is almost over and I'm losing blood circulation to my hands."

"Well, if you can't do the time, my best guess is you shouldn't do the crime," I joked. I nudged MacGuffin with a smile but he was too busy staring at Becky Lipgloss, who was quietly whispering to Amber Holiday. I looked back at Evan who was scowling at me from the stocks.

T-Bone shielded his mouth and whispered to Evan, "Quiet, kid! You know you have to stay in character!" He turned back around to us with a wide, fake smile. "Moving on!"

We approached the waterfall that was behind the Triple Crest hotel. The noise of the great falls was deafening, which drowned out the sound of T-Bone's voice.

"And here is Triple Take Falls, one of the most important stops on our tour. It is said that those who pass through the waters never return. At least, they don't return the same." T-Bone put his sunglasses on to shield his eyes from the reflection of the sun on the water.

"It's said that the gold everyone was looking for was somewhere beneath the waterfall. Only General Kettle knew for sure. Hundreds of people have died searching for that gold, never to find one nugget." T-Bone stepped back, took a breath of fresh air, and let it out. "Now, this way to the most historically important stop of the tour—the hotel gift shop."

CHAPTER 3
Stuck in a Plastic Past

We were left in the gift shop to buy something
that was like "buying a piece of history"
according to T-Bone. That was true if history
was made up of fake swords and snow globes.
The place was full of toy rifles, bows, and arrows.
There were white wigs and General Kettle
costumes lining the walls.

I poked MacGuffin with a plastic arrow to get
his attention. "I'm starting to think this whole

field trip has been one big ruse. They round up all of us kids, teach us a whole lot of nothing, and then ask for all of our money. What did you learn from the tour?"

MacGuffin shook a snow globe and watched as the white flakes fell over Triple Crest. "Well, I got to thinking," he said. "If this place is the home to a historically significant battle, then I would bet that this is a hot pocket of paranormal activity."

I shook my head and made a *tsk* noise at MacGuffin. "Poor Mac. I thought you were better than that. There are no such things as ghosts, ghoulies, or any creepy crawlies. We are detectives. That makes us men of logic."

"Psst," I heard. "You, kid, come here," said a skinny, older fellow behind the counter. He had long, white hair. But the top of his head was bald. He also had a long handlebar mustache that matched his white hair. He pointed his bony index finger at us and motioned for us to come toward him.

I walked toward the counter. "Gee, sorry, mister. I didn't mean to make fun of your merchandise. I was just making a point to my partner here that there are no such things as phantoms or spirits." I nudged MacGuffin and looked back up at the cashier.

"The name is Hanna—Mr. Hanna. And I haven't been here long, just a year or two. I came here to be General Kettle in the reenactments." He patted his flat stomach. "Unfortunately, they didn't think I had the right look." He sat forward. "But there are ghosts, all right. Plenty of 'em," said the old cashier. "There are ghosts of the old Triple Crest townsfolk, pirates, and even General Kettle himself! They are looking for one thing and one thing only. It can finally put their souls to rest."

MacGuffin leaned forward, practically going over the counter. "What is it?"

Mr. Hanna leaned even closer to MacGuffin's face. "Gold, boy. The gold." The old cashier sat

back in his chair. "To be honest, those pesky ghosts have kept business here darn near to nothing for the last couple of years. All we get are locals and," he looked us over once more, "school field trips."

MacGuffin took a few steps back and pulled me with him. "Hey, Jon! Maybe this is it! Maybe this is the mystery we can solve," he whispered.

"Look, Mac, I told ya," I said, "I'm not doing any cases that involve ghosts. It just doesn't make sense to me."

"I'm not saying the ghosts are real. What I'm saying is there is something that is keeping people away from here, like the man said! If it's ghosts, then fine." MacGuffin looked around and then back at me. "But what if we stumble across that gold?"

That certainly got my attention.

"The gold, Gummyshoes," MacGuffin said. "What if we happen to find that? What a reward that would be if we came across it!"

I stopped MacGuffin there. "You know that what we do is for good, not gold."

"What about Little Ricky? You can get him out of the dog pound, no sweat!" MacGuffin took a step back. "But you're right. This isn't a case about ghosts or gold. It's a case to find out what has put this town into the dumps. We'll help the citizens. That's all you want, right?"

"Maybe you're right, Mac," I said. "Maybe we can do right for a whole town! What's driving the business and tourists away? Could it be ghosts? You can bet your stars that we'll prove it isn't!"

I saw MacGuffin's eyes change focus from me to someone behind me. Then I felt a warm breath on my neck. I turned around to see Evan from the stocks earlier. But now he was wearing normal clothes.

"What was that out there, huh? You think you're better than me or somethin', kid? You think you're better than history?" he barked, staring directly into my eyes.

"Listen, pal. Whatever this is, it isn't history,"
I said. "This is all some story thought up to make
this place more important than it really it is."

Evan became red in the face. "I'm so sick of
city kids like you coming up here to our small
town thinking you are above all of this." He
picked up a plastic blacksmith's hammer. "I could
be out, cruising with my pals, having a great time.
But I choose to preserve history so everyone can
understand that we all come from something."

My eyes went from the hammer up to Evan.
"All right, bub. Do what you have to do for a buck.
That's none of my business. All I'm saying is
that people get so wrapped up in history that it's
impossible to see what you have right in front of
you." I looked around the gift shop. "I mean, look
at this stuff. Why would you want to stay stuck
in a plastic past? People even think this place is
haunted, for crying out loud."

Evan put the hammer down. "This place is
haunted all right. You have no idea how many

ghosts roam the forests of Triple Crest. Ghosts of pirates and townsfolk all trying to get revenge for their lives lost in this town. Each trying to find the lost gold."

MacGuffin stepped in. "We're detectives, pal. We base our work on logic and intrigue. If we don't see it, we don't buy it."

"You don't believe me? Fine. Go 100 yards into the Black Forest just east of Triple Take Falls. If that's not enough to make you believe, friend, I'll drop my beef with you and move on."

I grabbed a Triple Crest history pamphlet off of a shelf. Evan pushed an angry breath out, turned around, and walked out of the gift shop. I read through the history pamphlet and studied the map trying to find exactly where the Black Forest was.

I wrote down what Evan said in my notebook. That's where I keep all of my important clues. This seemed like a case that might be pretty interesting to solve.

Just then the bells on the gift shop door jingled as Principal Ant opened it and walked in. "All right, class, finish up your purchases and meet me and Principal Links outside. We're going to leave to get some lunch and then come back to Triple Crest." He turned around and the bells jingled as he exited.

We walked out to meet the two principals. And the students got onto their separate buses.

CHAPTER 4
See You in the Future

I ended up being last to board the bus. That meant the only seat left was next to Principal Links. He was thumbing through a book he bought at the shop. It was about the Battle of Triple Crest. He stopped on a picture of a heavyset man with a long beard wearing a uniform.

"I didn't know Santa Claus fought in this battle, Principal Links," I said, bouncing up and down with the bus.

"That's not Santa Claus, Gummyshoes," Links

said. "That's General Kettle, who led the people of Triple Crest to victory against the pirates. Kettle proved that freedom, not just gold, was worth fighting for. He was a brilliant man who had no intention of being in the army. And yet he made history."

"History, history, history," I complained. "That's all I'm hearing. I have a feeling that once we're ten miles outside of this hole, no one will even mutter the word history. It's nothing the Internet can't teach us."

Links shook his head. "You know what, Gummyshoes? History tells us a lot about the present." He closed his book and looked at me. "Just think about that."

I looked out of the window. "I've thought about it, Chief. And all I can say is I'll be seeing you in the future."

Principal Links crossed his arms. "Yeah, well, I bet you didn't know that General Kettle was a misunderstood boy himself. People thought he was going to grow up to be nothing but a menace. But he proved them wrong."

The conversation was clearly going nowhere, so I did my best to change the subject. "So, Chief. I'm interested in knowing *your* history with Principal Ant," I said. "You guys were chums back in the day, correct?"

"Well, Gummyshoes, if you must know, Marcus and I were close friends back in school," Principal Links said. "We disagreed on a project we did together in high school. It was a History Day project, in fact."

I rested my head against the bus seat. "What was all the fuss about?"

Links turned and looked out the bus window. "It was actually about Triple Crest."

Just as I was about to get the dirt, we pulled into the restaurant parking lot. The buses emptied and we got in line for our boxed lunches. I grabbed mine and went to a table to sit and eat. After I finished lunch, I looked over the Triple

Crest history pamphlet. And I took out my notebook, too. I read through my notes, adding more as I thought about the case. Were there really ghosts in the forest? After a while I found my walkie-talkie, pushed the talk button down, and spoke into it.

"Mac! Mac, are you there?" I asked.

I waited a second and heard the other voice come in.

"10-4, you've got MacGuffin," he said.

"Well, listen. I've been thinking...," I said.

"About the case?" MacGuffin asked.

"You got it, pal," I said. "And there's no time like now to start."

"What do you have in mind?" he asked.

"When we get back to Triple Crest, let's split from the group," I said. "Then we can go explore the Black Forest. Let's see these ghosts for ourselves."

CHAPTER 5
Entering the Black Forest

When we got back to Triple Crest, MacGuffin
and I snuck away. The only person who noticed
was Frankie. He followed right behind us.

"You boys ready to find some ghosts?" I asked
with a chuckle.

"Anything to keep Frankie busy," MacGuffin
responded without a smile.

My attention went from Mac to Frankie.
"Hey, Frankie, buddy? We need ya for this case.

It's a really important job." I pulled an extra flashlight from my back pocket and switched it on. "I'm gonna need ya to stay out here in front of the woods. Make sure no one comes in or out until we come out." I flipped the handle of the flashlight in midair and grabbed the shining end, holding it out to Frankie. "You think you can do that?"

Frankie took the flashlight out of my hand and examined it. "Gee, Jon, do you really mean it? You want me to be a part of this case?"

"Sure do, bud," I smiled.

"I'm the man for the job, Jon," he said. "I mean it. I won't let you down."

I took out my flashlight and switched it on, examining the area around us. "I know you won't, Frank." I turned the light on MacGuffin who was switching on his flashlight. "Well, away we go then."

MacGuffin and I made our way through the Black Forest. It was very dark once we entered the forest. The woods were thick with trees and shrubs. It wasn't easy and I was beginning to think it might even be dangerous.

"So, what's been happening with your gal, Becky Lipgloss?" I asked, trying to make the forest a little less scary.

"She hasn't really talked to me lately. I figure the big holiday dance we're having next month will be my time to make a move. We're not getting any younger, you know," MacGuffin replied.

"You're right, Mac," I said. "We aren't. That's why I think you should make your move sooner. Why not during our field trip today? History, from what I gather, is rather romantic."

"Take it from me, Gummyshoes," he said. "It's not that easy. People have been talking."

"Talking? Talking about what?" I asked.

"Well, people say that you and I have been creating trouble," he said. "That we have a history of causing a lot of chaos around the school."

"People get wrapped up in the history of things, even when the stories aren't true. You know for yourself that it isn't us! We are the ones who are helping students!" I shouted.

Mac started walking again and I followed. "I think it's just best if I cool it with the detective stuff for a while," MacGuffin said. "I mean, just until the stories die down a bit. I don't want to be remembered like this, Jon."

"Then what is this, Mac? What do you call this—a *non*-case?!" I asked.

"I call this my last case. But mostly it's just two friends going into a forest to see if there are any ghosts." He pointed at the trees. "I still want to be friends with you, Jon. But after this case, you're going to have to work without me."

Just then, I looked behind my shoulder to see that Frankie still had his light fixed outside of the forest. Ghosts—what a bunch of hooey. I took one more look behind my shoulder to see that Frankie's light was now missing. *Well, so much for that.* Then I heard a twig snap a few yards ahead and grabbed MacGuffin's arm.

"Shh! Did you hear that?" I whispered.

We heard another snap. Then I heard what sounded like a young child laughing. That brought the creepiness factor up to the maximum.

"We better skedaddle, what do you say, chum?" I whispered to MacGuffin.

"I say you're right," he whispered back.

We turned around and both of our flashlights landed on what looked like General Kettle. He looked exactly like the portrait in Principal Links's book, only sadder. His skin was white like snow and he had black bags around his eyes. He opened his mouth as if he was about to say something, but instead he let out a terrible

moan. MacGuffin and I let out bloodcurdling screams and split in two separate directions.

I ran as fast as I could, jumping over logs, sticks, and puddles. The flashlight was going every which way.

"RUN, MAC! RUN!" I screamed.

I tripped over a twig and my flashlight flew out of my hand and went under some leaves. I stopped and tried to slow down my breathing. I knew I was standing somewhere near where I came into the forest. I could not see much, though. I heard a twig snap and some heavy breathing behind me. I knew for a fact that it was not MacGuffin. I kept running. I made it out of the Black Forest and kept running, even when I could not hear anything behind me.

What in the frozen bananas was that?! I thought. *It couldn't have been. It wasn't a—I mean, it's not possible, right? A ghost? A real ghost? Well, it was in front of me somehow. Staring into my eyes.*

I stopped running once I was in the middle of the field. I was covered in cold, hard mud. Twigs and leaves were stuck to my hair and jacket. I panted, trying to catch my breath. I looked back toward the Black Forest and saw no flashlights. He got him. General Kettle's ghost got my best friend.

Then I felt a push from behind me.

"GUMMYSHOES!"

I screamed in horror and turned around to see that it was MacGuffin.

"Mac, you're okay!" I looked around. "Where's Frankie?!"

"I saw him running off when he heard our screams," he said.

We stood there, staring at each other for a few moments.

"You saw what I saw, right?" Mac asked.

"I sure did," I replied, still trying to catch my breath.

"So, what now?" Mac asked.

"So now," I said, pulling a broken stick out of my hair, "we go hunting for a ghost."

CHAPTER 6

Like Owner, Like Dog

We got back late in the afternoon from our field trip. I was so worn out that I went straight to bed. I woke up the next morning on top of my covers, with mud dried on my clothes. It was Saturday and the sun was shining brightly through my window. I put my hand down to where I thought Little Ricky would be to give him a scratch behind his ear. Only there was nothing but sheets. *Drat.*

I took my time getting out of bed. I was sore

from running in the forest. I took a long, hot shower. I had a lot to think about. I had to figure out a way to get Little Ricky out of the pound. I had to solve a case while a ghost roamed the woods trying to scare the pants off anyone who entered. And MacGuffin was ending our partnership.

Once I had a plan, I hopped out of the shower and put on clean clothes. Then, I dialed MacGuffin.

"Mac, meet me at Ice Man's in twenty minutes. We have a lot to talk about," I said into the phone.

"You got it," he answered.

I threw on my jacket and stepped outside, closing my eyes and letting the sun hit my face. When I opened my eyes, I saw a big, white truck driving down my street. I'd know that truck anywhere. It was Animal Control Officer Tommy Donkers. Donkers stopped his truck a few houses down and got out with a net in his hand.

Donkers had some height to him. He certainly wasn't intimidated by small dogs like Little Ricky. He had a white button-down shirt that was covered in mustard stains. It was tucked into white pants that had grass stains on the knees. His dirty blond hair was short in a buzz cut. He was chasing a little dog around the lawn trying to scoop her up in his net. The little dog was Caps, Amber Holiday's dog. That didn't seem right, so I decided to go pay him a visit.

"Caps is allowed on this lawn. She runs around it every day," I said, casually walking up to Donkers with my hands in my pocket.

He stopped running around like a goon. He stood with his back to me and the net in his hands.

"Animal control officer duties include investigation of stray or unlicensed dogs and the removal of said stray or unlicensed dogs," he said, turning around to face me. "Much like your mutt, what was his name? Little Roger?"

I made my hands into fists within my pockets. "It's Little *Ricky*," I replied through my teeth.

"Right, Little Ricky," he repeated with a serious look on his face. "Animal control officer duties also include the enforcement of *all* county codes and state laws that pertain to domestic, as well as wild, animals." He twisted the net between his hands. "And Little Ricky, unfortunately, didn't feel like he had to follow those county codes or laws."

"Yeah, he's also a dog," I replied.

"Tough noodles, kid. Little Ricky was unlicensed when I found him digging up City Hall's flowers. The penalty for an unlicensed dog is $300. As they say, like owner," he sneered, "like dog."

I took a lot of cold air into my lungs, held it for a few seconds, and then let the steam rise out. I turned on my heels and just walked away. The thought of Little Ricky sitting in one of those dingy, dirty cages at the pound was unbearable. I had to do something. I thought about what I was going to do all the way to Ice Man's. I pushed the door open to the sound of a full house. I made my way through the crowd and found Mac sitting at a table for two.

"What's the matter?" MacGuffin asked.

I thought for a few seconds then came back to the conversation. "Hmm? Oh, nothing. Just a lot on my mind right now."

"The ghost of General Kettle?" he asked.

"Well, that's a start, I guess. What do we know? We both saw him, so we know it wasn't a dream." I waved to Ice Man for two scoops and took out my notebook to review the clues. "The old timer said he thinks it's the ghosts that are keeping the business of Triple Crest in the dumps. But what is driving the ghosts to do so?"

MacGuffin watched the scoops of ice cream being placed on the table, and then looked up at me.

"The gold," he said.

"The gold, friend," I said with a smile.

"So, what?" he asked. "We need to find out if the gold exists?"

"Oh, it exists, all right," I said. "And we're going to find it. We have to. In the name of Little Ricky and the people of Triple Crest. We will find the gold and offer it to the ghosts as a way to put their souls to rest."

MacGuffin took the plan in for a few seconds. "Okay, then how are we supposed to find the gold?"

"That's simple—I'll become an insider at Triple Crest, MacGuffin," I told him with a grin.

CHAPTER 7
Getting into Character

Later that day, I went back to Triple Crest.

"So let me get this straight," said Mr. Hanna at the Triple Crest gift store. "You want to volunteer here. Why?"

I took a step closer to the counter. "Frankly, sir, the field trip I attended yesterday inspired me to dive deeper into the history that surrounds me. I feel like if I don't have an understanding of what's happened before me, then I won't fully appreciate what's in front of me."

The old timer sat back in his chair and scratched his beard. "Well, it's always good to see youngsters gaining an interest in our town's history." He thought and scratched for a minute more. "And we had to let our usual actor, Evan, go yesterday for breaking character."

He stopped scratching and looked me square in the eyes. "That's one thing we do not tolerate here. You must be in character at all times. If not, you get the stocks. You hear?"

"Loud and clear, sir. So whaddya say? Can I volunteer?" I asked.

"You sure can, son. Go suit up and meet the rest of the actors back here!" Mr. Hanna said. He reached over the counter and gave me a solid handshake.

The plan MacGuffin and I devised at Ice Man's had been set in motion. I was going to enter the town and get as many clues as I could to figure out where the gold was. It seemed simple enough. We'd help out a town in need and I'd be able to get Little Ricky out of the slammer in no time.

I put on the costume that the old timer gave me. It wasn't really my style—a long-sleeved, white button-down shirt with a white vest. My pants were black wool that only went to the top of my knees. I wore long white socks that went up to the bottom of my knees and black shiny shoes. I looked in the mirror and chuckled at myself. I took the tri-point hat and placed it on top of my head, completing the look. As I gazed into the mirror, I noticed the rack of other costumes behind me.

I walked down the line of clothing, inspecting all of the outfits. Peasants, soldiers, and blacksmiths—everyone was there. I stopped on a familiar costume. It was one I had seen before, but I just couldn't place where. I had soaked up so much history in the last day it felt like it was all meshing together. I noticed dried mud on the costume's pant legs. I decided to make a note of it in my notebook.

Outside, the sun was shining brightly and the

actors who played the townsfolk of Triple Crest were going about their day. I walked down the main street, taking it in. I went past the butcher shop and the general store. People were doing what they were supposed to be doing. And they were all staying in character. I walked up to a woman wearing a long, puffy blue dress and bonnet.

"Excuse me, ma'am. I'm new here and I was hoping you could help me," I said tipping my tri-point hat.

"Well, sure, son. What can I do for you?" she replied with a smile.

"I was wondering if you could tell me where all of the gold under this town is," I said casually with a wider smile.

She lost her smile and looked forward. "Son, you should know that no one knows where the gold is." She looked around and then back to me. "The last boy asked too many questions and got locked up for it."

Everyone really has to be in character here. No one is supposed to know where the gold is, just like in the past. I guess I was on my own searching for this treasure. But wait, what did T-Bone say? General Kettle was the only person who knew where the gold was. And if only one person knew where it was, then that person had to be hiding it. I had to find Kettle and give him the shakedown.

I knew I had to keep in character or I would get locked in the stocks. As I turned to leave, I saw the man himself—General Kettle. He stood before a group of townsfolk and was addressing them with a speech.

"People, we know that the pirates will be approaching soon. As we prepare, let us not forget that our beloved Triple Crest was built with good neighbors and hard work. We should live our lives, not our history." General Kettle looked around at the townsfolk. "When the sun sets and hits just right, you will see just where the gold lies—in our souls. We will not be prisoners of the gold." The crowd applauded him and then he was gone.

Then it hit me. I remembered that it was odd that Evan was always locked up when he was so serious about being historically accurate. He must have been getting in trouble on purpose. But why? The stocks would not help me find answers. I had to go to the jail.

I saw a tour group being led through the main street by T-Bone and I knew I had to take my shot now. I pulled out my walkie-talkie and placed it to my ear.

"What? You can't be serious, MacGuffin! I didn't know that's how the big football game turned out!" I said, making sure the entire group of tourists saw and heard every last word.

T-Bone stopped mid-sentence and let his jaw drop to the ground. I looked over, gave him a wink, and then continued talking into my walkie-talkie. "I know, TV is so bad lately."

T-Bone motioned to a soldier behind me, who grabbed me by the shoulder. "Young boy, you will have to come with me."

I was in serious trouble. I threw my hands in the air and walked away with the soldier.

CHAPTER 8

Where the Gold Lies

We marched all the way into the jail. The soldier placed me in the cell and then stood outside it. "One historical error gets you the stocks," he said. "Two gets you time in jail. You are charged with two historical errors. The charges are use of future technology and having a conversation about future sporting events."

"You mean present technology and sports?" I asked from my cell.

"No! This is the 1800s for crying out loud.

There are no walkie-talkies or football yet!" he said.

"Ha! You said *yet!*" I cracked.

The soldier looked flustered, so he turned around and left. I stood in my cell and looked around. I had three walls and a set of bars in front of me. The ground was nothing but dirt. This is what Little Ricky must feel like at the pound right now—poor pooch.

When the sun sets and hits just right, you will see just where the gold lies—in our souls. The sun was setting and I waited to see where the gold was. What if General Kettle didn't even know where the gold was? What if he was just as big of a phony as the rest of the people in Triple Crest?

As the sun was setting I noticed the light through the open window move from the top of the wall behind me, slowly to the bottom. The sunlight finally stopped, right on top of my shiny black shoes. *When the sun sets and hits just right,*

you will see just where the gold lies—in our souls.
Not *souls—soles*! The soles of my feet!

I started kicking all of the dirt on the ground until the tip of my shoe found it. I got down on my knees and started brushing all of the dirt away. It was a trap door! I unlatched it and saw a wooden ladder that led down. Evan was close to the gold, but not close enough. I heard a major commotion coming from outside the cell window. I ran to it and got on tiptoe to see what was going on.

As I shielded my eyes from the sun, I could see a man riding into town on a horse. He was screaming something. It was something I couldn't understand clearly. It sounded like he was saying the pie is yummy.

People crowded together on the main street were waiting for the man to come closer. The man on the horse finally made it past the walls of Triple Crest and did not slow down. He rode as fast as he could, past all of the fake townsfolk and real tourists.

"The pirates are coming!" he screamed.

I realized it was the beginning of the reenactment of the pirates' attack. It would be the perfect distraction for me to go missing from jail. I got back to the ladder and started to climb down. Once I hit the bottom, I pushed on in the semi-darkness. It was like a hallway made of stone. There was not a whole lot of room to walk, but it was enough to make my way through. Walking forward, I started to hear a noise. It sounded like water—a lot of water.

After a few hundred yards the noise became really loud. It was like a mad storm whipping through the cave. I realized it was Triple Take Falls. Only I was at the bottom of it! I could see the sun setting through the water. But the sunset wasn't my biggest find. No, the water falling from above was landing on gold—lots and lots of gold.

I had done it. I had found the gold that Evan and the ghosts of Triple Crest were after. Finally the town could be restored to a normal, historical spot and I would be able to get Little Ricky out of the pound and away from Tommy Donkers.

I couldn't possibly take all of the gold out of there on my own, so I picked up a bar of that glimmering gold and held it in my hand. It was light, so I put it in my pocket and ran back to the ladder that led up to the cell. I got to the top, closed the trap door, and waited.

Eventually, the noise of the pirates' invasion died down and I heard the applause of the tourists. The same soldier who had put me in jail came back and opened the cell.

"You're free to go," he said as I got up off the ground.

"Well, that's good. I don't know how much more time I could have spent in this jail," I said.

"No, I mean, you are free to go from this job. You're done volunteering," he said, closing the cell behind me.

I changed out of my costume and thought about my next move. I was going to have to contact the ghosts somehow to give them some gold. That meant that I had to see the ghost of General Kettle one more time.

CHAPTER 9
Let History Rest in Peace

MacGuffin joined me by the Black Forest soon after I was released.

"You sure you want to do this?" I asked. "I can do this on my own."

"This is my last case, Jon. I plan on seeing it through," Mac answered, switching on his flashlight.

We marched on into the forest and I listened, hoping to see the ghost of General Kettle.

"So, you are sure we can just hand the ghost this bar of gold and hope he leaves?" Mac asked.

"If I'm right, which I can say with confidence that I am, then yes. I think it will be that simple," I responded. Suddenly, we heard a twig snap.

"Shhh, I think I heard something," Mac quivered.

I stood straight and waited. I heard it, too. Then the sound of a child's laughter went through the woods. I pulled the bar of gold out of my pocket and held it out. "Is this what you wanted? Then come get it!" I screamed into the darkness.

One more twig snapped. We turned around to see General Kettle standing in front of us. He was white as a cloud. He didn't look the same as he did alive, at least, not like that actor who played him. I guess it was a little much for MacGuffin, because he went stiff as a board and passed out. I just stood there with the gold in my hands.

"Here it is. Put your soul to rest now, General," I said, laying the bar of gold in front of me. "Or, is it Mr. Hanna?"

This stopped the ghost from moaning.

"How ... how did you...," the ghost stammered.

"It was rather simple, actually, if you look at the facts," I said, putting one of my hands in my pocket and walking back and forth. "You came here a year or two ago with gold on your mind. You heard all of the stories and read the history. You knew it was here, it had to be." I kicked a rock aside and kept talking. "You grew out your mustache and groomed for the part. But, like you said, you didn't quite have the body for it."

Then Mr. Hanna pulled three stuffed pillows out of his uniform jacket and dropped them on the ground.

"That meant you could never know the true location of the gold, because like everyone else in this town, you must always be in character. So you recruited someone to be on the inside.

Someone who was historically passionate, yet wanted people to be far away from here, too." I pointed my flashlight at a tree behind Mr. Hanna. "So you got Evan in on the scheme."

Sure enough, Evan walked from behind the trees. "Evan was smart. He figured out from General Kettle's speech that Triple Crest isn't a prisoner of gold, the gold was in the prison!" I went on. "But he couldn't do it. You can only be sent to jail if you get two historical errors. You couldn't get past one, could you?"

"It's easy to fake history for city kids like you. You don't understand how hard it is for me to upset the truth," Evan snarled.

"That's my second point," I continued. "You both had reasons for the ghost charade. Mr. Hanna could scare off anyone who wasn't local from finding his gold. Evan could make sure that the only people who truly appreciated history would stick around. You both got something out of it."

Mr. Hanna wiped the white make-up off of his face. "Okay, fine. You figured it out. What do you want from us?"

I pointed at the gold bar. "I will tell you exactly where the gold is and how to get to it. But I want you two to leave Triple Crest. Let history rest in peace. No more ghost stories."

We all agreed and I told them exactly how to get to the bottom of the jail without leaving out a detail. We shook hands and they both left. I bent down on one knee and slapped MacGuffin awake.

"Mac, it's done," I said.

"Yeah? What happened?" He asked in a dreamy haze.

"We won't be seeing those ghosts anymore," I told him.

"Ghosts?! You mean there were more than one?" Mac asked getting off of the ground.

"*Were*, chum. But they're history now," I said.

CHAPTER 10
Good as Gold

A week later, Mac and I, with Little Ricky in tow, found ourselves back at Triple Crest. We did another tour with T-Bone and this time it was fascinating. People from all over the country were coming to see the historical Triple Crest and Triple Take Falls. I had never seen so many people before.

"I gotta admit, Mac. Having actually lived through this, I find the whole story to be really interesting," I whispered as T-Bone went on about the General Store. "I could see myself becoming a major history buff if this was our last case."

MacGuffin stopped as the rest of the tour went on. "Well, I think this case has helped me see that what we do is important, with or without anyone else's definition of history."

I slapped Mac on the back. "You said it, chum."

"I can't believe Mr. Hanna and Evan fell for the fake piece of gold," he said.

"It was all fake, Mac!" I said. "With a little research, I found out that the gold was discovered and taken out of the cave decades ago. The underground waterfall was even part of the tour! Evan just never got down to it because he was always locked up in the stocks."

We started walking behind the tour again.

"So those two are just stumbling around, weighing down their pants with fake gold," Mac chuckled.

"As Triple Crest gets to peacefully live out the past," I said, finishing his sentence.

"I guess it was a case of two fellas who were just too wrapped up in history to see what was actually in front of them," Mac said. "It's a shame that gold was fake, though. Imagine having all of that loot!"

"Ah, don't worry about the loot," I told him. "We made out okay. We did right by a whole town! And we didn't have to bail Little Ricky out of jail."

"How did he get out of the slammer, anyways?" Mac asked.

"Well, it turns out that Donkers was looking for some gold of his own," I said. "He intentionally ripped up the flowers in front of City Hall and blamed Little Ricky so he could get that $300 fine. He was caught on security cameras doing it again last week."

"Looks like his job is history, then," Mac smiled.

"Indeed it is," I laughed.

Mac and I both stopped when we had realized that T-Bone had stopped the tour and was watching us talk.

"Is there anything you two would like to add?" T-Bone asked with his hands on his hips.

I looked to Mac and then the rest of the group. "Sure, I think there is something I could mention. I learned here that a great man once said you should live your life, not your history. And I have to admit, that advice is as good as gold."

X Triple Crest dressing room: costume with mud on the pants.

X Actor said: "The last boy asked too many questions and got locked up for it."

X Why is Evan always locked up?

X General Kettle actor: "When the sun sets and hits just right, you will see just where the gold lies—in our souls."

Triple Take Falls

Hotel

Gifts | Jail

Coffee Shop | Smithy

General Store | Butcher

Black Forest